Wish
Twisted Tales of Familiar Faces
Courtney Konstantin

M4L Publishing

To my readers...that follow me and read whatever's next!

Shadows of Agra Heights

THE BUSTLING CITY SOUNDS of Agra Heights flowed down the dark alley. None of the men dressed in business suits, or women in high heels, paid any attention to what or who was in the shadows. That was how Alan liked it.

Peering out from his makeshift tent, he watched as people rushed in all directions, hurrying to get nowhere important. For him, his little camp contained everything that mattered. There was a time he believed he would be one of those men in a rush, but war had warped his mind so greatly that even seeing the sun for too long could cause PTSD flashbacks.

The police had carted him off plenty of times since he returned from the never-ending war. His ranting caused too much of a disturbance for shiny Agra Heights. The powers that be in the city didn't want to be reminded of the war to which it had dispatched its citizens.

Enlisting when he was eighteen, Alan was full of hope and dedication, believing he would be defending those who couldn't defend themselves. What he found was that he had a knack for being an assassin, and he was liberally used in that way. After serving his eight years, all he was left with were skills that couldn't legally be applied in the real world and debilitating PTSD. It felt like a lifetime ago, though in reality, it had only been a couple of years.

Alan had to drag himself from his camp, though, to search for food and water. One way he gathered what he could was by finding an inconspicuous place to panhandle, hoping that some of the business types had bleeding hearts. He always wore the old worn military jacket that had covered him in faraway places. It seemed to drum up the most sympathy.

With his head down, to avoid any gaze that might set off his anxiety, Alan wove quickly through the throng of people, until he could enter the park a few blocks from his camp. Here, he allowed his eyes to rove the green trees and the beauty that was the perfectly manicured park. Flowers of every color popped up in perfect beds, surrounding the bases of trees that were older than Alan, and probably older than his parents as well.

He found his normal corner to sit on the ground. A spot on the asphalt that put him out of the path of the people walking by, but not hiding him so much that they could just ignore his presence. He pulled his jacket close around him and pulled up the hood of the zip-up sweatshirt he had underneath, hiding some of his face. Not making eye contact with those moving around him was the best way to keep his mind settled and not lose himself to something that wasn't actually there.

Soon, the sporadic sounds of coins falling into his old paper coffee cup tinkled in his ears. He didn't look inside the cup to count what he was receiving. Even if he only made a dollar for the day, it was enough to buy an old sandwich at the corner deli. And that would be better than eating the old food they threw in the dumpster in the back alley. He tried to not hope, but Alan's mind wandered to better, warm food, with a warm drink to go with it.

He had been homeless long enough that even his stomach seemed to understand the situation and rarely ever made noises when he was hungry, which was most of the time. It wasn't an easy life for Alan, but he preferred the streets and his own private camp to anything the asylums or the jail cells could offer. He wouldn't even willingly stay in those places for the three guaranteed meals a day.

A pair of dirty loafers that looked like they were begging to be cleaned, stopped in front of Alan's spot. He didn't look up. Didn't acknowledge the person. He had been heckled, physically attacked, and yelled at. You name it, someone had probably done it to Alan in the park. He didn't want to make it easy on the person, so he refused to look up, to give them his gaze.

Instead of one of the many scenarios Alan had in his head, the man wearing the dirty loafers crouched and carefully put down an old bottle next to his cup. Alan still said nothing, didn't look at the man, as he hesitated, his hand still on the neck of the bottle. It had no legible label, but Alan guessed it once held wine. The glass seemed thick, so the liquid it had carried was probably expensive and potent. Alan didn't want it. He was about to say that when the crouching man spoke.

"I'm sorry."

The words were soft and then he was gone, merging into the traffic of the park walkers, cyclists, and dogs on leashes. Alan stared at the bottle and then tilted his head to look up, only to catch the back of the man moving away. He was picking up speed, practically running. His clothing didn't seem to be any better than his shoes, but Alan could only see the back of him. He never even looked back at the homeless man he had spoken to.

Alan wondered what the words meant, but he left the bottle where it was. He didn't touch any of the charity until he finished for the day, as was his custom. He continued to keep his eyes averted and nibbled on bread that was past its sell-by date. His hands were dirty, and he studied his nails, thinking about how he needed to sneak to the pond in the park and clean up a little.

When dusk fell and the rush of the foot traffic died down, Alan gathered his belongings. He packed up the blanket he had sat on all day and stretched his back and legs. He put the cup with the change and the weird wine bottle into his pack. One thing he learned while living on the street was to never let his neighbors see his haul for the day. Someone was liable to walk off with it.

Thinking about the dirt under his nails again, he detoured deeper into the park. There was a walkway on one side of the pond, while the other side was lined with trees. Alan had long ago found a pleasant path through the trees that took him closer to the water than the bridges across the way did.

Checking his surroundings, he made sure that he hadn't been followed and that no one was watching him. He couldn't ease the paranoia that lived in his mind just by checking his surroundings. Finding a large enough pile of leaves and sticks, he hid his pack near him, but out of sight of anyone that could stumble upon his hidden area. He patted down the leaves and made sure a few sticks stuck out at awkward angles, so it looked natural. His fears caused him to spend more time on the camouflage than was necessary, but he couldn't help it.

Satisfied with his work, he slowly approached the water's edge. He bent and plunged his hands into the murky water. It was likely not much cleaner than him, but it was cool and made him feel like he was doing something about his hygiene. There were times he attempted to stay in shelters, especially for the hot meals and the showers. But they were too busy, packed with the bodies of people just like him. Even if he could find an open bed, he could never handle staying for long.

Alan rubbed his clean hands against his dirty jeans, but the dirt wasn't under his nails any longer and that helped calm his anxiety. He was more careful with digging out his bag, flicking his gaze from side to side, as if there were enemies behind every tree. The dim light that the sun was still giving off, even as it fell below the horizon, caused the shadows to lengthen and take on shapes Alan didn't enjoy thinking about. With his pack on his shoulders, he hiked out of the trees at a fast pace, trying to outrun whatever could be in the shadows.

It felt like he had held his breath until he got back to his campsite. His little part of the alley was closed in using old mattresses, tarps, and cardboard. He had nothing of value to steal, because everything worth anything was in his pack. But he was still careful with how he set everything when he left, little booby-traps that would tell him if someone tried to enter his domain.

Once he confirmed everything was where it should be, he ducked inside and took a deep breath. His space was as it should be. Even without actual walls like a true house, Alan felt safe here. It was the only home he had known in months. His paranoia had given him plenty to work on over the days when he wasn't looking for food or sitting in the park. Without family to speak of—his parents had long since given up on him—there was no one in civilized society to wonder where Alan had disappeared to.

In the darkness, Alan found his stash of half-burned candles. He was careful with the flame, by keeping it in a glass jar and away from anything that could catch. Once he had a small light in his tent, he carefully undressed and changed to a set of clothing he saved just for sleep. He left his backpack, deciding to deal with the money in the morning.

As he laid his head on his makeshift pillow, he heard a howling. It sounded far off, as if the wind was blowing between buildings, though nothing moved around him. The night was still. Alan lay on his back and stared at his tent roof, his ears straining to hear the noise again. When it didn't come, he rolled and fell into a dreamless sleep. The howling came again, but Alan didn't wake. He was dead to the world. Even as something shifted in his backpack, causing it to fall over.

Mist and Madness

THE NEXT DAY, ALAN sorted through trash in his alley. It was trash day, so the businesses often put more into the large dumpsters to prepare for pickup. Alan tossed things aside, looking for something edible. The leftovers of a half-eaten snack bag of chips went into his mouth as he kept searching.

"Hello?"

A soft voice called outside the dumpster, causing Alan to freeze. Technically, he wasn't breaking any laws, but he wasn't interested in a fight with someone.

"I saw you get in there. I live across the street and can see into the alley. I brought you something," the feminine voice called again.

Embarrassment struck Alan as he thought about a woman seeing him climb into the dumpster. Normally, Alan didn't have a problem doing what was necessary to survive. He wasn't ashamed of the life he led. He also rarely had any interactions with people that could comment on his state of disrepair.

Knowing the woman was still standing there, just on the other side of the metal container, waiting for him, made Alan look over the lip of the dumpster. His breath caught when he saw the most beautiful woman he had ever seen. She wore jeans and a sweater, but he could tell they were expensive pieces. She held a foil-covered plate in front of her, and he noted her delicate fingers.

"I won't tell anyone, and I'm not going to hurt you. I just wanted to bring you some of the food I made for breakfast," she said.

She held out the plate, but Alan didn't move to take it. It was hard for him to trust anyone that offered kindness to him without wanting something in return. In his mind, he wondered what the woman wanted.

"I'm Badora. But people call me Addie."

Alan didn't respond, just shrugged, focusing his eyes on his feet. She said nothing, and he didn't look up as her pristine white sneakers stepped back from him.

"It's okay. I'll just leave the plate here."

Her footsteps receded, and Alan looked up to see the plate sitting on a stack of boxes across the alley from him. Looking toward the entrance of the alley, he saw Addie exiting, without looking back, her long black hair swinging behind her. She checked traffic, jogged across the street, and entered a building. Alan knew there were condos on the upper levels, but he never looked up. That wasn't a life he knew.

Though he was uncomfortable with how the food came to him, he took the plate and quickly went back into his area. He closed himself off inside the tent, making sure that even Addie, if looking down on him, couldn't see him. Sitting down with his back against the cold stone wall, Alan carefully unwrapped the plate. The scent of bacon wafted up into his nostrils, and he felt shocked by the clenching in his stomach.

With little thought, Alan ate. The flavors of the food burst on his taste buds, reviving long forgotten memories of eating proper food. When he went to the shelters he got hot food, but it was always over-processed and cheap. Addie had brought him real meat, fresh bread, butter, fruit and scrambled eggs. When he finished, his stomach was comfortably full, and he did not need to continue searching the dumpsters.

The priority of food was out of the way. He turned to sort through his pack. He removed the dirty wine bottle and the cup with his collected money. Setting them down, he went for the money first, counting it twice. It was enough for a coffee, one of the few pleasures he still allowed himself. He hid the money in an inside pocket of his jacket.

Focusing on the bottle, he slowly turned it over in his hands. The glass was heavy and worn, with nothing but a faded and torn label on the outside. Alan couldn't make out what the label said, but he realized it didn't matter. The bottle was empty. It wouldn't have been the first time someone left trash for him when he was panhandling.

Still, something about the dark glass, almost unnaturally black, pulled Alan in. He wondered if it would clean up and be shiny and beautiful. When he shook it upside down, nothing but sand fell from the inside. He smirked, not surprised at having the bottle left for him. Most people saw him as someone not worth more than the trash he lived around.

Alan viewed the bottle, even though it was trash, as something that could be salvaged. Something that could be beautiful and useful once again. He didn't overlook the similarities to how he wished his life was. As he buffed the outside of the bottle with a cloth, the dust disappeared, and the black showed through.

A thicker spot of caked-on dirt made Alan scrub harder at the surface. He didn't notice the black mist at first that seemed to leak from the mouth of the bottle. However, once the dirt was cleared away, the black poured out. Alan dropped the bottle, causing it to fall onto his bedroll and slide toward the wall of the tent.

As the tent became full of the writhing black cloud, Alan threw out his arms, trying to find the walls. Desperately, he scratched at the vinyl, looking for a zipper to release him from the horror that was filling his home and seeping into his lungs. He continued to look for an escape, as tendrils of the smoke scraped across his scalp, face, and neck. When he tried to push away what was touching him, his hand went through the blackness. Nothing solid existed.

"What is this? I need out!" Alan cried.

Nothing answered, not that he expected a voice to come out of the black. He could no longer see anything inside the tent. When he held his hand up in front of his face, he waved it around and couldn't see his fingers until he was touching his nose. He tried to crouch lower, close to the ground, but the mist didn't seem to care if it was near the ground or rising into the sky. It continued to move, like a hundred black snakes, slithering around him.

Alan cried for help, but the mass closing in on him swallowed his voice. He blinked furiously, hoping to clear his vision, but it was as if he was suddenly blind, with no source of light. He shoved his fists into his eyes as he collapsed to the floor and rocked.

When he stopped rubbing his face, he realized there was a faint orange glow. Looking up, he stared into two orbs of orange flame. They danced in the middle of the blackness, staring down at him. He blinked again, imagining what he was seeing was a figment of his imagination created because he didn't want to lose his vision. But when he opened his eyes wide, he was still seeing the fire orbs.

The longer he stared, the closer the orbs got, until the fear was more than he could handle. He opened his mouth to scream, but the black smoke wriggled toward him, filling his mouth and invading his lungs.

Suffocation came swiftly, and Alan tried to cough and gag. He heard a deep, growling chuckle as his body rebelled against the invasion of the smoke.

"Hello, slave."

The words resounded in his head in the same deep voice as the laughing he had heard. As the smoke moved into his body, the tent lightened and a second later, it was as if it had never happened. Alan lay on his back, gasping and hacking, as if he could eject the black mist from his organs.

Instead of anything coming out, he could feel something foreign slither through his veins, pumping with his blood as it familiarized itself with him. Alan rolled and tried to push up to his hands and knees, oxygen slowly coming back to him. He didn't know what was happening, but he needed to get his bearings.

"This body will do nicely."

Those growled words were the last thing Alan heard before his body collapsed in the middle of his tent. His eyes closed, his subconscious fleeing as his being no longer seemed to be under his control. Even as he lost the world around him, he could feel the black fog in his mind.

Through Her Eyes

ALAN HAD LOST ALL concept of time. When he awoke, deep confusion and fear struck him as he looked at his surroundings. He was in the park, but instead of mid-morning like he last remembered, the moon was now high in the sky. He lay awkwardly near the pond where he normally cleaned. Though he told his extremities to move, he still didn't seem in control of himself.

Feeling he had little choice in the matter, he continued to lie still between the trees of the park. He gazed up at the sky, but the darkness reminded him of what had happened in his tent and the oily feeling inside his bones. He squeezed his eyes shut against the memory and the feeling that was still with him.

Slowly, control seemed to come back, as his fingers, and then toes, moved. Gradually, he adjusted his position to sit up and observe his surroundings. The darkness of the park didn't scare him nearly as much as before the incident. Now the light that shone from the moon felt comforting and grounded him in the place he was.

He pushed shakily to his feet. His body canted to one side until he threw up a hand to catch himself against a nearby tree trunk. It was then he saw the skin of his hand and his confusion deepened. Leaning toward the tree trunk, he brought his face closer to his hand. When he still couldn't be sure of what he was seeing, he pushed off the tree and stumbled until he fell to his knees in a pool of moonlight.

In the dim light, the skin of his hands shone, a dark liquid drenching every inch. In some areas it was dry, in others it was still an oily slick across his skin. At first, he imagined it was the same darkness that had assailed his body. But he then realized it wasn't completely black, but such a dark red that it could only be one thing.

Panicked, Alan rushed to the edge of the pond and plunged his hands into the water, scrubbing at the caked material that covered him. He pushed up the sleeves of his ratty button-up flannel. The red spread from his hands, over his wrists, until it finally tapered off below his elbow. There was no doubt in his mind that he was covered in blood.

He ripped off his flannel, realizing it, too, was wet and covered in blood and gore. His mind couldn't connect what the appearance of blood meant. Where had his lost time gone? The fine hair on the back of his neck stood, and he whipped around, expecting to see someone watching him. Nothing moved between the trees or in the shadows.

With his hands back in the water, he continued to scrub until he was sure all the blood was gone. He shivered, from the cold, or from the fear, he wasn't sure. His teeth chattered as he slowly tripped his way through the park. The place he loved was a different mosaic at night. His mind was too muddled to take in what he normally never experienced.

Once he was finally back in his tent, he threw his flannel, crumpled, into the corner. He didn't want to look at it. He just wanted to hide his head in his sleeping bag and forget the day happened. His bedroll wasn't the most comfortable bed in the world, but for him, it was the comfort he needed.

Sleep didn't come. Every noise outside his tent made him jump. He could see the black bottle, lying where it had fallen during the day. Staring at it, he remembered how he had heard someone, something, speak to him from the black fog. But he couldn't understand the words he had heard, or where they had come from.

"They came from me, slave."

Alan shot up in bed, hearing the deep voice that was edged with a growl. He looked around the tent, reassuring himself that he was alone.

"You are not alone, not any longer."

"Where...where are you?" Alan stammered.

"Look inside. You will find me," the voice said in a whisper that Alan could actually feel in his brain, as if the sound came from within.

"What are you? Why can I hear you inside my mind?"

Instead of speaking, images flashed inside Alan's mind. Memories, landscapes, events he had never seen personally. But as he saw them, it was as if he was there and had taken part in them. Horrific events of murder, famine, genocide and more filled Alan's mind. He gripped his head between his hands and squeezed his eyes shut, though he couldn't push out the pictures.

"Stop! Stop! Why are you doing this?"

"You are my new slave; thus, I can do as I wish."

"What are YOU?!" Alan screamed.

New images flowed into Alan's mind. First was a small lamp, ornate and golden. It reminded Alan of something found in the ancient Middle East. A black smoke appeared, as if it flowed from inside the lamp. When it stopped, a large cloud, similar to what Alan had seen in his tent, floated above the lamp and a man appeared, watching in wonder and some fear. Then, Alan watched as the orange flame eyes appeared and even what looked like a body could be seen, flame raging in its chest.

The monster and the man with the lamp exchanged words. But Alan wasn't privy to what they said. Instead, he watched as the monster shot forward and went up the man's nose and into his mouth. The man clawed at his throat, falling to his knees as he coughed. Alan's hand rose to his own throat, remembering exactly how that felt.

When the scene ended, the beast inside him spoke again. "I am what you see."

"You came out of the bottle, out of the lamp before? What are you? A genie?" Alan asked, speaking out loud, though he knew his thoughts could be heard.

Before a reply came, white-hot pain shot through Alan's brain, as if he could feel his arteries bursting.

"That's such an insulting term."

Gritting his teeth, Alan tried to fight against the pain, but he wondered if this was the end of him.

"Then what term should I use?" he finally could say.

"I am what is called a djinn."

Alan searched his knowledge. He wasn't sure what a djinn was, but it seemed to be similar to a genie that lived inside an inanimate object.

"Doesn't that mean you grant me wishes? All you have done is infect me and make me lose a day. And what about the blood?" Alan asked.

The pain inside Alan's head lessened, and he could release the pressure he had on his temples. He felt the laugh of the djinn slide inside his subconscious, and the feeling made Alan shiver.

"You only know the myths that the djinn has spread over the years. We worked hard to make sure the weak minds of humans were not afraid of us."

Alan knew he was feeling afraid now.

"What happened to me today?" Alan asked, done with the background information, still feeling like there was blood under his nails.

A pleasure-filled sigh passed through Alan's mind before the djinn spoke again.

"You worked as my slave, that's what happened yesterday."

"Yesterday?" Alan asked, but he wasn't sure he wanted the answer.

"You assumed only the day had passed. But alas, I have been with you two days."

Alan shot off of his bedroll and paced. He had lost two whole days. How was that possible? His body didn't feel like his own. He didn't remember eating. He couldn't remember using the bathroom.

"All of those things are trivial, slave. I instructed you to do the things your body required. I need your body healthy."

"For what?" Alan whispered, afraid of what the djinn's plans were.

"Whatever I please, slave."

"And what did you please yesterday?"

Alan realized he had stopped speaking out loud. He just thought the question and the djinn could hear him. He didn't find that aspect thrilling, and it made him feel even crazier.

"I will show you."

A feeling of sleep came over Alan, but instead of finding himself in a dreamless state, he found himself walking through a dark parking garage. Overhead lights dimly lit the area, but he immediately noticed that many of them were burned out. But that fact wasn't surprising to him, because somehow, he knew the garage, and he was walking to his car. Though Alan hadn't owned a car for years.

He looked down to find keys in a hand that didn't belong to him. The nails on the hand were long, acrylic, painted a deep blue. Alan's subconscious jolted, trying to make sense of what he was seeing and feeling. Everything felt familiar, yet he had never been in the parking garage he was walking through.

He looked beyond his hand and saw that the body he was looking out of was female. She wore a well-fitted suit jacket and matching skirt, with a white blouse. Her shoes were mile-high heels, the kind Alan always wondered how women kept their balance in.

The sound of the heels clicking against the concrete floor echoed throughout the garage. There was a sense of tension, and Alan realized the woman was nervous and on guard as she walked through the garage. But it was a walk she made every day, and he knew she was being unnecessarily paranoid.

Without warning, a dark shape stepped from behind a large van, blocking the woman's path. Alan was shocked to realize that he was staring at himself. The woman's body froze, and she stared at the man that had appeared out of nowhere. Alan could feel her hesitant smile as she continued without speaking. A moment later, she was knocked off her heels and fell face-first toward the ground.

A cry came from her lips, and she felt her wrist twist as she tried to catch herself. Pivoting, she caught herself on her shoulder and could look back and see what had happened. Alan stood over her, his form looming over the small woman. Looking from the woman's eyes, Alan barely recognized himself. His face was screwed up in a furious scowl, and hatred shone through his eyes.

Staring at himself, he saw his brown eyes glow a faint orange. It wasn't Alan staring down at the woman; it was the djinn, looking through him.

When Fear Feeds

"WHAT DO YOU WANT? Money? I have money in my purse. Take it."

The words came from Alan's mouth, but it was a woman's voice that echoed in the quiet garage. Alan's form didn't respond. Instead, his eyes continued to glow, and the woman's scream was high and loud as it looked like orange flames were leaping from Alan's orbs. She knew, without a doubt, what stood in front of her wasn't of this world and fear flooded her veins. Alan could feel it all, as if he had lived it himself.

Then the woman was grabbed by the ankle. She twisted, trying to grasp hold of anything to stop the man from taking her. Her acrylic nails scraped against the ground, popping off, causing her to cry out in pain. The concrete was rough and dug into her hips as she tried to turn and flail away from Alan.

Behind the van, where Alan's body had been hiding, was a bag. It looked like something a handyman would have carried, clearly stolen because Alan had never seen it before. Once the woman was with him behind the van, Alan flipped the woman until she was on her back. Her screaming intensified, and she kicked out, trying to strike out with the one heel remaining on her foot.

Alan's free hand rummaged in the bag and a roll of duct tape appeared. The woman knew what was coming, and the struggle increased. When the man leaned toward her, even Alan in her mind, started to plead and beg to be let go. The words were ignored as he forcefully pressed a strip of duct tape against her mouth, smothering them. Alan felt the struggle to breathe, the fear of suffocation, the stickiness of the tape against her face. He was living it all.

Inside Alan's mind, he begged the djinn, not with the woman's voice, but with his own.

"I don't want to see this. Please stop. It's enough!"

The djinn ignored him, and Alan felt nothing but the woman's mind with his own. His experience continued to be out of body, as the woman fought and rolled, trying to get away from his own form. The orange flame caused a glow to illuminate his face and the woman on the ground. Alan wanted to lend his strength to her, to help her get away, to change the fate that was closing in.

Lost in the woman's mind, Alan missed the moment his own body reached back toward the bag. The next thing he knew, the woman's desperate need to escape had increased and metal flashed in the orange glow. A serrated utility knife was in Alan's hand, and with increasing panic, the woman watched as the blade came toward her.

Inside her mind, his mind, Alan screamed. He cried and tried to force the woman's body into movements that weren't part of the memory. There was no doubt that what he was seeing was a memory. It felt real, tangible to his subconscious. Even though he didn't remember the actual moment, he knew he had lived it.

The knife cut through the woman's shirt until it was buried in her abdomen. Alan's form moved slowly, with deliberate precision. The pain assaulted her senses, causing her eyes to widen and halting her muffled scream. Alan's hand twisted the blade, causing blood to bubble up around the metal. The woman seemed to find renewed strength, and she bucked her body, pushing Alan's form back.

Alan, in the woman's mind, cheered for her. He could feel every second of pain and panic, the emotions his own, as he tried to assist the woman in breaking free. She scrambled to her bare feet, just for seconds, before Alan had the knife blade pressed to the soft flesh under her chin. She froze, the threat clear. Blood trickled down her stomach, soaking into her suit skirt and running down her thighs.

There were no words spoken. The djinn didn't speak, but the woman was pulled back into the darkness. It was the last thing the woman would do, the last moment of fight she had in her, before her life was ended. As he watched his own face over the woman's, his own hands digging into her body cavity and separating her organs as the djinn instructed, Alan felt as if death had taken him as well.

As the memory ended, Alan experienced a sudden jolt of consciousness, as if he had been immersed in an ice bath. The tent was awash in sunlight, letting him know he had lost more time. He rushed out of his tent and barely made it into the alley before he bent and vomited. Bile splashed against the building wall and on his shoes. As he looked down, he noticed that the blood of the woman had also splattered his shoes. The woman he had murdered.

He toe-kicked off his sneakers, sending them across the alley, where they crashed into one of his mattress walls. Stumbling away from his puke, he spun in a circle, panicking about someone finding him a murderer. At the end of the alley, people moved as if they had no idea of the blood on his hands. Taxis, buses and cars drove along the street, without a care. All the while, Alan's mind was slowly degrading.

"Why? Why would you do that?" he cried out, forgetting he could just speak in his head.

People on the street paused, but easily dismissed him as a crazy homeless man.

"I feed off the fear, slave."

"Why do you need me? Just do whatever you want, without me."

The djinn's voice was a deep growl as he spoke. "I do not have a physical form. Whoever has my dwelling becomes my physical form."

Alan spun, looked at his tent. The djinn had come from the bottle that a strange man had left. Rushing back into the tent, he grabbed the bottle and went back into the alley. He stared at the bottle and looked at the brick wall across from him. Pieces of a plan formed, and he raised his arm when a voice broke into the alley.

"Are you all right?"

He froze, recognizing the voice and not wanting to look back. He didn't speak, but slowly lowered the bottle.

"I saw you throwing up. Are you sick?"

"Turn around," the djinn said in his mind.

"No. Leave her alone," Alan replied in his mind.

"Sir?" Addie called from behind him, her voice drawing closer.

"Go away," Alan called over his shoulder.

There was a pause, and he didn't hear her footsteps leaving. Without thinking, he glanced back, and he knew the moment the djinn saw her. He slithered across Alan's brain as if he was about to tunnel in. Alan clenched his teeth and glared at Addie.

"Leave me alone! Go! I'm not your charity case. Get away from me!" he screamed.

A sad look crossed her eyes before she made her face go blank. She nodded once and turned on her heel. As soon as traffic was clear, she jogged across the street and entered the building across the way. He was glad he didn't know where she lived exactly. She was safer as far away from him as possible.

Anger rose in Alan, and he furiously flung the bottle across the alley, so it slammed into the brick wall. It shattered and fell into pieces on the ground. He huffed as if he had just run a mile, staring at the pieces of the bottle, waiting for something to happen or change.

Nothing happened. For a few minutes, everything was silent. The djinn didn't comment on the broken bottle. Alan couldn't feel him. Closing his eyes, he tried hard to settle his heart so he could hear something other than the thudding in his ears. He focused on the sound of traffic, his even breathing, people on the phone as they walked by.

A quiet scraping sound caused goosebumps to break out across his skin. The djinn moved through his mind, and Alan released a pained moan. He was still there. Opening his eyes, he jumped back when he found the shards of glass moving across the concrete. They snaked toward each other, an invisible force powering their movement. Once they were near each other, there was a small spark before they connected again.

"No, no, no, no, no," Alan moaned, shaking his head in disbelief.

"Did you truly believe a broken bottle would rid you of me?"

A Touch of Kindness

THE REST OF THE day was lost, but not because the djinn took over his body. Alan sat in his tent, his mind racing and fear fueling him. The djinn stayed silent, as if it knew how close Alan was to a breakdown. He did nothing but stare at the tent wall. The bottle had completely repaired itself, and it sat where Alan had thrown it.

Alan remembered the man leaving the bottle. He had apologized. That convinced Alan that the man was well aware of what he was leaving next to the homeless man in the park. The man who left the bottle had to be the djinn's previous victim. He had tried to run away, through the crowd of the park. As if something was trying to follow him.

Alan tried to remember what the man looked like, if there were any identifiable logos or brands on his clothing. But he couldn't remember a thing. Alan had been so busy trying to blend in, to not draw attention or make eye contact, he hadn't looked up in time to see anything of value.

The man's action of handing over the bottle gave Alan an idea of what he needed to do, but he realized this would entail handing the curse off to someone else. Someone else would do the murders and suffer the way he had. It wasn't something he could bring himself to do, not yet.

He knew there had to be another way. He just needed to find it. And to do that, he needed to learn more. For some reason, he felt alone, as if the djinn had taken residence in a dark recess of his body and was just waiting for his next outing. Alan wasn't sure how long it would last or what type of freedom he had.

Quickly, with little clear thought about what he wanted to do, Alan put clothes on. The clothes weren't clean by any means, but they weren't stained with blood, which was the best he could wish for. He walked out of his alley with a clear goal in mind, and the djinn seemed to let him go. He didn't dare look back at the shiny bottle sitting against the brick wall.

Two miles later, Alan entered the library. He had been there several times since he became homeless. The librarians were mostly kind about him using the bathroom or reading books inside when it was raining. So, when he entered, he smiled softly at the woman behind the counter, who waved at him as if they were best friends.

It didn't take long for him to look up the subject "djinn" on the catalog computer. He pulled a few books from the shelf and went to a back corner that had a large recliner and coffee table. It was blissfully empty and just the way Alan liked it. He set his books down and looked around to make sure he didn't have anyone watching him.

He froze when he looked down the aisle he had just come from. Standing, observing him from around a corner, was Addie. She had clearly followed him to the library and was watching him look at a stack of books about Middle Eastern folklore. Realizing that Alan had caught her spying, she moved toward him.

"What are you doing here?" he exclaimed in a low whisper, his eyes glancing around again to make sure there was no one else.

She shrugged. "You were sick earlier. I was worried."

"Why are you so worried? I'm no one to you. Just a man living in a tent across the way."

She shifted uncomfortably, and Alan was struck again by how beautiful she was. If he was someone different, in a different world, she would be a woman he would want to pursue. But this was the life they were living, and by the look of her clothing the few times he had seen her, she was well out of the league of a man living on the streets.

"I've seen you feeding the cat that lives in the alley with you. You're a kind man. Just because you live in a tent doesn't mean you don't deserve someone to look out for you."

He was speechless. How long had she been watching him if she had already seen him feeding his cat? The animal wasn't exactly his, but he had named him Boo, because he was solid black, like a cat from Halloween. Once he had fed Boo twice, he started coming back each day around the same time. Alan made sure he had some sort of lunch meat, or even tuna from a can if he could afford one. He couldn't handle the cat starving.

"What's your name?" Addie asked.

"Alan," he replied without thinking.

She tilted her head before saying, "I'm going to call you Al. Alan feels so formal. You don't seem formal."

Alan had once been called Al, as a high school student. But it never really stuck, and no one really paid enough attention to call him that again. Hearing it from Addie gave him a warm feeling that he didn't want. Her inquisitive gaze moved away and slid to the books he had stacked on the table. Without invitation, she moved and picked up one of the books.

"Middle Eastern legends. Interesting topic."

"You can go now," Alan said.

He wasn't typically a rude person, but his worry about the djinn coming forth and doing something horrendous to the beautiful woman was overwhelming. He couldn't feel the monster, but he felt panicked about having a dream of Addie's death at his hands. She represented purity and kindness. He was losing himself, but he couldn't lose that.

"I could help you. I love reading and learning."

"Don't you have somewhere else to be?" Alan asked.

"Not really. My father doesn't let me work, so I'm left with my educational pursuits."

Alan couldn't fight his curiosity about her.

"Why wouldn't he let you work?"

"You've probably heard of him, Khalid Haddad? Well, most people know him as Rick Haddad," Addie explained.

She didn't look over at Alan when speaking, her cheeks turning pink. He wasn't sure why she seemed embarrassed by her father's name, but Alan had never heard of him. Alan was also not very familiar with much of society. When Alan didn't reply, Addie looked over and raised an eyebrow.

"You've never heard of him? Well, that's refreshing. Mostly when I meet people, they're looking to get to my father somehow. They think he can help them, give them a job or do them a job."

"He sounds important," Alan replied, since he wasn't sure what else she wanted him to say.

"He thinks he is. A lot of others think so too, I guess."

"But you don't?"

"I don't want anything to do with his dark business." Addie's face took on a serious look, and Alan knew she was a bright spot in an otherwise crap world.

He was unsure of what to say to her again, and it frustrated him. He was torn between wanting her to stay, to tell her the truth about the djinn, to ask for her help. But the rational part of him that was full of fear knew he was risking her life by having her anywhere near him.

Standing next to her, his homeless state was even more clear. He tugged at his dingy T-shirt and fidgeted, waiting for her to make her own choice to stay or go. She set down the book that was on the top of the pile and turned to face him fully.

"I know I make you uncomfortable. I'm sorry, I'll go. Just remember, I live right across the street. You can ask the doorman for Badora Haddad, he'll find me. I'll let him know you're okay. I mean, only if you want to. Okay, I'm going to stop, I'm just rambling. I'm sorry."

"You said I'm sorry, twice," Alan mumbled.

She looked at him, and her face broke into a bright smile. It loosened the tension in her brow and made her even more incandescent. "Was that a joke, Al?"

"Maybe," he sheepishly replied.

"We're going to be friends. You don't realize it yet, but we will be."

She stepped around him, and her hand squeezed his upper arm before she walked back down the aisle toward the entrance of the library. His arm felt warm from her touch. He stood still, longer than he should have, thinking about Addie and how she had touched him without thought. He couldn't remember the last time someone bothered to check on him or didn't cringe at his nearness to them. Addie was something else.

The Djinn's Hunger

BEFORE ALAN FINISHED READING the books he had found, the library was closing. Not one reference to djinn talked about murder or being possessed. During the entire time Alan spent with his nose in the books, the djinn was silent and unmoving. It made Alan wonder if the monster needed to sleep or recharge after he forced Alan to do his bidding.

On the way back home, Alan stopped at a small convenience store and used the two dollars in change he had in his pocket. He bought a small bag of chips and ate them while he continued his walk home. It wasn't enough, but it helped keep his stomach from growling loudly.

He was surprised to find a paper bag outside his mattress wall when he got to his alley. He glanced over and found that the glass bottle was exactly where he left it. The shiny nature of it didn't blend well with the dirt and trash that littered the rest of the alley. But it didn't seem to attract anyone else to take it away. He wondered for a moment what would happen if the trash company took it.

Carefully, he leaned over until he could see into the paper bag. A folded piece of paper sat on the top and he pulled it out.

Just in case you decided you wanted my help – Addie

He couldn't stop himself from looking over at the building her condo was in. There were a lot of lit up windows, but he couldn't possibly tell which was hers. He had to wonder if she was watching him now. With that in mind, he waved at the building, as if to thank her for whatever was in the paper bag.

Without looking inside, Alan picked up the paper bag and moved into his walled off area, cutting himself off from view. He set it down gingerly, as if it were breakable. It was easy to tell that Addie came from money, had plenty of it to live in the fancy condo. A bag of food was likely nothing to her, but to Alan it was everything.

He pulled out a loaf of bread, a container of charcuterie type meats and a small package of cheese. There was a large bottle of water, as well as a bottle of soda, a luxury item that Alan never purchased for himself. The last thing he found was a small can of cat food. He felt warmth spread across his chest. Appreciation for Addie thinking of Boo. The cat would come around shortly for his dinner, and Alan was happy to have something filling for the animal.

After he enjoyed the meal, saving most of the bread for another time, he started his nightly routine of checking around his area and making sure Boo was off for the night. A woozy feeling came over him, and he felt something shift inside him. Panic struck him and he ran to zip himself up in his tent. He doubted that would stop the djinn. Alan was still not sure what would stop the creature from taking away his freedom.

"Running does no good, slave."

The voice made Alan jolt. The djinn had been silent most of the day. He tried to push all thoughts from his mind, not wanting his secrets or his investigations to be revealed. But the djinn seemed to sense what he was doing.

"You will find none of the answers you seek. History does not understand my kind."

"Just go. You can go back into the bottle," Alan pleaded.

The voice in his head deepened as anger flared within the djinn.

"Life in the dwelling is near death for djinn. I will not go back. I will feed. Maybe on the female friend you have."

Alan pushed Addie from his mind. He didn't think about where she lived, what she looked like, or the feelings she created within him. He brought forth a scene of war, something he normally never focused on in fear of causing his PTSD to become uncontrollable. The djinn seemed to delve into the memory, soaking it up, enjoying it. Alan felt sickened by the way the djinn actually found pleasure in the horrors he had experienced.

"Your mind is the perfect playground for me, slave. I think I shall stay awhile."

For the first time in years, Alan felt like he just wanted to weep. He had seen countless people die throughout his time at war, even friends that fell at his feet. But his eyes never became wet. Now, as the despair hit him in the chest, he couldn't think of anything else to do but break down.

He laid his head down on his bedroll and wrapped his sleeping bag around him. The chill he felt wasn't from the night, but from the evil that leeched into his body. The djinn slid through his veins, an evil sigh of contentment echoing through Alan's mind. Even while living on the streets, Alan prided himself on being a good person.

"That is one of the best things about finding you. It is most fun to corrupt those with a pure heart." The djinn responded to Alan's thoughts, as if he had spoken them aloud.

Alan squeezed his eyes shut, hoping for a night of sleep and not murderous memories. Over the months he had been living in the alley, he had gotten used to the sounds of the surrounding city. There was never a moment of silence. He had never wished for quiet more than he did at that moment.

The sound of pounding feet passing his tent wasn't something new, but the feminine scream that followed was. The djinn rose, restless at the sound of fear in the woman's scream. Alan tried to force him back down, into whatever dark part of his soul he could keep him. He slowly sat up in his bed and tried to listen.

"Get off of me! Help!!!" the feminine voice screamed.

Alan leapt into motion, immediately positive he knew the voice.

"Help! Asshole! Get off me!"

Alan burst into the alley from his living space. Deep in the shadows near the end of the alley, he could see a struggle happening. He ducked into the darkness next to the wall and followed it toward the people. A grocery bag lay on the ground, its contents spilled across the alley, confirming who was being attacked.

When he reached the scuffle, he found Addie, fighting with all her might against two large men that looked to be hired muscle. One had an arm around her from behind, trying to pin her shoulders to him as he attempted to drag her back toward the entrance of the alley. The other had been trying to grab her feet, but as she kicked out, the man caught a heel to the cheek. He howled in pain, and Alan cheered internally.

Alan's instincts were kicking into high gear, instincts he had worked hard to suppress. The things he had learned and done weren't moments he was proud of in his life. He did his job in the military, did what was required of him, even when he didn't completely agree with any of it. That time left him with skills, honed for fighting and defending himself and others.

The group approached the darkened section where Alan hid. As soon as the man, who was still trying to grab Addie's legs, was within reach, Alan struck. His first blow was to the man's knee, knocking him sideways off his feet. The crunch was loud enough that Alan knew he had done the damage he had hoped for. The man was still trying to climb to his feet, shock preventing him from registering the pain he should have felt in his leg.

When the leg crumbled under his weight, Alan took a running leap at him and struck him quickly on the bridge of his nose with a superman punch. Blood exploded from the man's nose, and he flew back, bouncing his head off the asphalt. Alan pivoted to find Addie and the second man staring at him.

The djinn took that moment to rise, recognizing the conflict. Alan growled internally, not willing to risk Addie's life, because the monster wanted to feed on human fears. His body felt frozen for a split second, and he wasn't sure he could even breathe. The djinn slid along his muscles, as if he were sliding under Alan's skin to inhabit each part of him. Alan focused on the man holding Addie, not allowing the djinn to see his interest in the woman.

Addie's hesitation ended before the man's, and she stomped down with her heel on the man's foot. He grunted and released her just long enough for her to drop to the ground and crawl away. The indecision from the would-be kidnapper was all Alan needed to deliver a swift kick to the man's groin. The djinn approved of the move and the kick was even more forceful than Alan could have done on his own. When the man fell, Alan reared back and punted the man in the face with the toe of his worn sneaker.

Both men lay prone on the ground of the alley, and Alan checked that they weren't getting up again. The djinn sighed, relishing the conflict and the blood that had been spilled. He felt satisfied for the moment and gradually disappeared into Alan's subconscious again. Rushing over to Addie, Alan crouched in front of her, hands out, waiting for her to realize who he was. Her eyes were wild, looking through him more than at him.

"Addie, you're okay. But we need to get you home. And you should call the police," he said, keeping his voice low and calm.

"No police. Need my father," she mumbled. She finally gripped Alan's outstretched hands and shakily got to her feet.

"What can your father do?" Alan asked.

"Make these men disappear."

When Power Collides

It was only three minutes before the doorman of Addie's building came rushing across the street. From under his pristine uniform Alan had admired more than once, a small pistol appeared. He carefully screwed on a silencer and motioned for Addie and Alan to move away from the attackers.

The quiet pfft sound from the gunshots was barely audible to Alan and was completely lost once they reached the entrance of the alley. The doorman came back to them, looking all business again.

"Ms. Badora, we really should get you inside. Your father is on his floor and is waiting for you to be delivered safely."

"I'm not leaving without Alan. He saved my life." Her small hands clutched his sleeve and Alan momentarily felt embarrassed by the state of the shirt he was wearing.

The doorman nodded and stopped the light traffic so that they could cross the road. At the door of her building, Addie went to pull Alan in, but he froze. Her questioning gaze turned back to him.

"I don't belong in there," he said.

He wasn't only thinking of his status as a homeless man, who just happened to live in the alley across from the beautiful building. Just that alone would stain the unsullied environment. But if Addie knew what lurked inside him, or if the djinn thought to use her against him, Alan couldn't bear either of those ideas.

"You belong wherever I am. You saved me, Al. I don't want to think about what could have happened if you hadn't come."

"It was because of me you were even out there. You were bringing me food, weren't you?" Alan asked.

Addie looked down, a slight blush to her cheeks.

"I knew what I had brought earlier wasn't enough for breakfast too. So, I was going to leave the bag outside your tent, so you had a meal in the morning." Her voice was soft, as if to hide her intentions from the doorman who stood with the door open, watching their exchange. She didn't want to embarrass him, and Alan felt himself softening toward her.

"Ma'am, it would really be best to get you off the street. If you and your friend would come inside," the doorman and undercover bodyguard said.

Addie reached out and grabbed Alan's hand, pulling him toward the door. He didn't move, but he met her pleading gaze.

"Just until I feel safe," she said.

He couldn't tell her no. For the moment, he lost himself in the feel of her soft palm against his rough one. He was too unclean for her, but he couldn't find the will to care about that. He nodded to her and stepped forward, entering a world that had always been beyond his reach.

His old sneakers squeaked against the perfect marble floor, as Addie led him across the lobby toward the bank of elevators. The doorman was sticking close to her, and he pressed a button that was separate from the normal elevator call buttons. Alan didn't question it, knowing he was just along for the ride.

A door opened, and it was an elevator off to the side that stood apart from the rest. Inside, Addie didn't let go of Alan's hand. He could feel her trembling, and he stood as close to her as he dared, hoping she would feel comforted. The elevator didn't ding on each level like normal buildings. It only opened when they reached the penthouse.

Alan tried to pull back from Addie, but her grip on his hand tightened, and she pulled him into the entrance of the penthouse. Looking at the building from the outside, Alan never could have guessed the top floor had vaulted ceilings, likely making it as tall as two floors combined. There were floor-to-ceiling windows, but he wondered what film was on the outside that made them unnoticeable from the street.

Two men approached them, wearing black on black suits, guns already palmed in their hands. The doorman nodded to them, and they had some sort of silent conversation. Then all three turned to look at Alan, standing slightly behind Addie.

"Who are you?" one man in black asked.

"No one," Alan replied.

Addie pulled him forward. "He's my friend, and he saved my life."

"Okay, no one. The boss wants to see you."

The men in suits turned, and Addie moved to follow. The doorman disappeared back into the elevator. Alan had no choice but to follow Addie further into the penthouse. The entrance was ornate, like places he had fantasized about in magazines. However, once they walked into the living room, he realized the entrance had been nothing.

Everything was white and gold. White marble flooring that had gold flowing through it. The couches that surrounded an indoor fire pit were white leather. The end tables were dark wood, with gold ornaments. In one corner, a white baby grand piano sat. A large TV was sinking into a hiding place in the floor, as if it were an eyesore that needed to be put away.

Alan had a hard time taking everything in. Once they entered, Addie let go of his hand and rushed to a man standing near the bank of windows. The way he embraced her, Alan could easily guess that the man was her father. The powerful, dark businessman was imposing and struck a solid figure in the middle of the living room.

"You're the man that rushed in to save the day? How did you know my daughter was under attack? Did someone send you?" Khalid Haddad asked.

Suddenly, Alan's arms were seized, one man on either side, holding him in place. Addie gasped and protested, but Khalid sliced at the air with his hand, silencing her.

"I will know how this came to happen directly across from our home."

Alan froze for a long moment, contemplating his options. Both men were armed, though they had put their guns into holsters under their suit jackets. Neither of them were holding him in a way he couldn't break out of, so he decided to wait it out until he no longer could.

"I didn't know anyone was going to attack Addie tonight," Alan replied, his voice even.

"He didn't, Father—," Addie started, but was cut off by a stern look from Khalid.

"You just happened upon the attack? That seems incredibly coincidental."

"It wasn't a coincidence. The attack wasn't my fault, but she was there because of me," Alan said.

Khalid shot a withering look at Addie, but she straightened her shoulders and lifted her chin. It was enough to make Alan fall for her even more. At that thought, he pushed it back, afraid of the djinn hearing his thoughts. Instead, when the djinn rose, it was in response to the anger Alan felt from being held against his will.

The djinn added to Alan's anger, causing the emotion to boil over and become uncontrollable. His vision became red, and he wasn't sure if everyone else could see the djinn through his eyes in that moment. Before he could yank the monster back, his body was moving. Without knowing what exactly he had done, one bodyguard fell, his hands cupping his crotch, while the other fell, grabbing at his throat, gasping for air.

The djinn roared inside Alan's head, begging for more, wanting to go further and hurt the guards again. As the one who had been kicked in the groin rose to his feet, Alan's leg shot out, landing a solid kick on the man's thigh. The guard collapsed with a cry of pain and stayed down.

All this happened in less than ten seconds, and Addie's scream caused Alan to stop all movement. With great determination, Alan pushed back the djinn, not falling into his desire to murder the guards. He turned, his sneakers squeaking against the marble sounding loud to his ears. Addie stared at him, her eyes wide. Khalid didn't move, only studied him with a strange expression on his face.

"You're an interesting homeless man. I've never seen one move quite like that," Khalid said.

Alan didn't respond because he wasn't even sure what he had done to take down the guards as fast as he did. He had learned several things during his time in the military, but his hand-to-hand combat skills were rusty at best. The guards were likely better trained than he was, yet they were no challenge for him. A sinking feeling in his chest told him it was because of the djinn's force inside him. The worst part was, a part of him, a small piece he wanted to deny, reveled in the power.

The Bottle Returns

It was his actions that night that created an opportunity Alan never expected. Khalid had anticipated some sort of attack. But that attack being against his daughter had not been in his scenarios.

A courier arrived at the penthouse the same night and delivered an offer.

"This man must be insane to think you'd marry me off just to make an alliance," Addie said.

Alan stood off to the side, still in the expensive high rise, yet not sure why he was there. Khalid hadn't excused him and the two guards he had taken down were told to leave and nurse their prides elsewhere. As Addie spoke, Alan watched Khalid's face closely. He immediately knew Khalid wasn't dismissing the idea as quickly as Addie.

"Father?" Addie's question broke the tense silence.

Khalid shook his head, but when he spoke, he didn't address her concerns.

"This man, your friend, will be your new guard. No matter what this message says, trying to kidnap you off the street is unacceptable. It seems you need someone full time."

Alan's mouth opened, but when he meant to protest, no words rolled off his tongue. Addie continued to stare at her father, waiting for his response to her statement. But Khalid did nothing but put his cellphone to his ear and summon an employee. A woman in a crisp white button-up blouse, navy blue pencil skirt and sky-high heels practically floated into the room.

Without looking at the woman directly, Khalid threw out instructions.

"Get this man into the condo next to Badora's. The one reserved for security. He will live there for the foreseeable future. Also, get him an employee credit card. I believe he'll need an appointment with Gio to be fitted with his uniform suits..."

Alan's mind was having a hard time grasping what was happening. Addie's eyes whipped back and forth between the three people standing with her in the room. She glared at her father, tried to implore with the woman, and when she looked at Alan, it was almost a sadness that crossed her gaze. He knew she wouldn't want to be stuck with a homeless man that she was just trying to feed once in a while. It made him stare down at his dirty sneakers.

"Sir, can you come with me?"

The woman employee had tapped her way over to him and was waiting for him to acknowledge her. When Alan looked up, she didn't smile, only held out her hand as if to ask him to walk ahead of her. He gestured with his chin that he would follow her, and she spun on her heel, quickly walking in her floaty way to the elevator. The last thing Alan saw as the elevator doors shut was Addie's sorrow-filled face.

The elevator was silent as it descended. He noticed that even the mechanics of the machine were a whisper, a perfect fit with the fancy building. When the doors opened again, they were in a long hallway, with doors on either side. The assistant strode directly to one, pulling out a ring of keys from some hidden pocket. Alan looked up and down the hall, trying to count the number of condos, but he couldn't see around the bend at the end.

The door in front of him opened, and the assistant didn't bother to ask him to walk ahead again. She strode in and stopped in the front room.

"This will be your place. Currently, it's stocked with all the basic requirements, but once you have your company card, you can buy whatever else you need. I'll make the appointment for your suits," she said, pausing to look him up and down. "You'll likely find new clothes in the main bedroom that will fit."

She started for the door, and Alan stood frozen in place, not sure where to go.

"Oh, I'll send some men to pack up your stuff. You were in the tent in the alley across the way, correct?" She didn't say the statement with any condemnation in her voice, only as if she were speaking an address.

Alan thought about his space and all the things he had accumulated in his years living homeless. A slight panic set inside his chest at the idea of losing it all. He just nodded to the woman, not sure what else to say.

"We'll put it in the basement storage until you have the chance to go through it and keep whatever you'd like to keep. Someone will be by later to give you more instructions."

And with that, she closed the door behind her, and Alan was left alone. The silence immediately closed in on him, and he missed his tent and the noise of the busy street. Wandering through the living room, he studied the open layout. The kitchen was off to one side, with a breakfast bar accompanied by two high stools. The living room faced it, with a large leather L-shaped couch.

Down a short hallway there was a half bath and coat closet. Alan opened the closet and found a few brand-new jackets of various sizes. He closed the door and continued his tour. The next door was closed, and he slowly opened it, finding what he assumed was a guest bedroom. The last door of the hallway was a larger than normal main bedroom. Alan slowly walked into it, but stopped. The carpets were pure white. Toeing off his sneakers, he moved through the room in his mostly clean socks.

As the assistant had said, there was clothing of multiple sizes in the dresser and closet. Alan ran his fingers over the clean jeans and T-shirts. The en-suite bathroom called to him, and he flicked on the light to an almost completely white marble room. There was a huge walk-in shower with multiple shower heads. A standalone tub sat next to it. Both were stocked with shampoo, conditioner, body wash, and loofahs. A drawer next to the sink provided a brand-new razor.

Looking in the mirror, Alan grimaced at his reflection. It had been weeks since he had shaved, and his beard was growing unevenly around his face. He could salvage his hair with a shower. It only took him a split second to decide that if this was his fate, he would take advantage of it.

Steam billowed from the shower stall as he stepped in. The water was hotter than anything he had felt in a long time. The showers he could get at shelters were usually lacking great water heaters and there was a large rotation of people looking to use the facilities. He stood under the spray for longer than necessary, allowing the heat to flow over his sore muscles. His skin was pink as he scrubbed it roughly, determined to wash away everything stuck to his body.

Once he was clean, he wrapped a towel around his waist and wiped the mirror so he could shave at the sink. He was able to neatly trim his beard using an electronic razor and then, using the disposable razor, he cleaned up his neck. He pushed his hair back and ran a brush through it. Just as he was setting it down, there was a knock at the front door.

Alan assumed it was one of Khalid's employees, so he rushed to the door. But when he pulled it open, Addie, with red-rimmed eyes, stood on the other side. Her gaze widened in surprise, and Alan could feel a blush on his cheeks.

"I'm...I'm sorry. I can come back," Addie said.

"No, it's okay. Come in. I mean, it's your father's place. Sit. I'll put some clothes on."

Alan stepped back for her to come in before he peered up and down the hall. After assuring there was no one around, he closed and locked the condo door. Addie had walked into the kitchen and was pulling a bottle out of a wine fridge Alan hadn't noticed. She held it up, and he nodded before heading back toward the bedroom.

His hands shook as he sorted through clothes to find something that would fit him. When he found what he thought were his sizes, he felt different. For years, he had worn whatever clothing he could find at a church or shelter. Nothing ever fit right. But now, the jeans were snug in the right ways and the T-shirt hugged him in the way most men wanted. Alan shook his head at his own reflection as he realized where his thoughts had gone.

Walking back into the main room, he saw Addie pouring wine in the kitchen. As he turned toward her, something on the dining room table caught his eye. He turned, and he stared, unable to blink or move. His heartbeat thundered in his ears as a slithering feeling under his skin caused goosebumps to ripple along his body.

"Did you think I would just disappear?"

The voice inside him almost caused Alan to fall to his knees. Instead, he continued to stare at the gleaming black bottle sitting on the table. Suddenly, Addie came from the kitchen and, seeing Alan near the table, walked toward him.

"Oh, I didn't realize you had a bottle opened," she said, as her hands reached for the djinn's bottle.

"No!" His body finally unfrozen, he rushed forward to grab the bottle before Addie's fingers could touch the glass.

Addie jumped back in alarm. Alan grabbed the bottle and stared at it. He wanted to fling it across the room, but he already knew that breaking it wouldn't do any good.

"Al?" Addie's uncertain voice pulled Alan back.

"I'm sorry. It's just, I...don't have an explanation. Sorry."

What could he tell her? That he was infected by a magical serial killer that had forced him to kill one woman so far. And it wasn't something he could control. How did he tell her he was afraid the same entity would zero in on her?

"She's not to my liking, slave. Not yet," the djinn whispered in his mind.

Alan didn't feel comforted by that.

Shadows of Control

"I'M SORRY YOU'VE GOTTEN dragged into this," Addie said.

They had settled on the leather couches, looking over Agra Heights through the large windows. Alan wasn't sure he could ever get used to seeing the city from so high up. When he looked down, he could clearly see his alley, and that explained how Addie knew so much about him.

"I'm sorry you seem to be stuck with me," Alan mumbled.

Surprise widened Addie's eyes as she sipped her wine and shook her head. "Not at all, Al. Honestly, you'll make me feel safer, I'm sure of it. My father just doesn't know how to be told no. And he didn't really give you much of a choice in the matter. I would never assume this would be the lifestyle you would choose."

"You won't insult me by pointing out I was living in a tent," Alan replied.

"Well, that doesn't mean anything—about you or what you did for me tonight. Thank you. How did you even do that? Did you learn to fight somewhere?"

"The military." He would not explain that he had done things to protect her and to take down Khalid's guards that he did not know how to do. The djinn had powered his body to do that.

Addie nodded, as if it explained everything, and Alan was glad he didn't need to explain further. Lying to the beautiful woman made his stomach go sour. They sipped wine quietly, and Alan lost himself in the taste of something he hadn't had in a very long time. Many people accused him of asking for money because he wanted alcohol or drugs. But he hadn't had a drink since he became homeless.

Alan knew his limits and after a few sips, he decided a full glass of wine would not be a good idea for him. He set down the half he wouldn't drink and stared out the windows at the night sky. It was late, and the events of the day weighed on him.

"I'm going to go. If you hadn't realized, my condo is right next door." Addie pointed toward the wall that her condo would share.

"What are your plans tomorrow? I guess we need to work out some sort of schedule if I'm going to be protecting you."

"After tonight? I won't be going anywhere. I think ordering food in will be the best idea. Would you like to join me?" she asked.

Alan nodded. He wasn't sure what he was supposed to be doing, but staying close to Addie seemed to be where to start. Private security had never been on his radar, and he wasn't prepared for the sudden thrust into the role. A part of him was worried about becoming comfortable within the fancy building, clean condo, new clothes. If he couldn't fulfill the duties Khalid was expecting of him, he would be back in his tent. He tried to tell himself he would be okay with that.

"I'm going to go home," Addie repeated, as she stood up with her empty glass.

Nodding, Alan stood and walked with her toward the door. When she walked out, he followed, and she shot him a small smile over her shoulder. He wanted to see which door was hers, to gauge the distance between their units. At her door, she pulled out a key and made quick work of the lock. She stepped inside and turned to face him.

"It's not that I'm upset about you being around, Al. Working for my father, with him, around him, isn't a normal job. It's probably going to be dangerous, and he's likely going to ask you to do more than protect me. I would really hate for something to happen to you because you were trying to help me."

He could see she was serious about her concerns, and he didn't doubt that she knew her father and his business better than most.

"I'll be careful," he finally said.

Addie smiled, but it was sad again, as she nodded her head once.

"Goodnight, Al. See you tomorrow."

He nodded and waited for her to close the door. Once he heard the locks click into place, he moved away. He counted the number of steps to his unit and committed the information to memory. Before going back into his condo, he walked along the hallway, counting the number of doors. On his mental list, he added that he needed to ask Khalid or his men how many of the condos were occupied.

Back in his condo, he shut the door and locked it. He stared at the lock for a long time, wondering how long he would live somewhere safe. As he turned toward the bedroom, his head spun for a moment, and he caught himself on the wall. The sudden desire to throw up hit him and he tried to get to the guest bathroom. The feeling of his skin crawling was the last warning he had before everything went black.

Consciousness came back to him in a rush this time, and he had little question about what had happened. He blinked his eyes against the bright light of the guest bathroom, where he was lying on the floor. Slowly, he took stock of his body. The feeling came back quickly, and nothing seemed to hurt. He stood and found the sink speckled with blood. Bloody shoe prints marred the flawless marble floor.

He followed them backwards, out of the bathroom, to find that they led to the front door. Anger and panic filled him as he thought about Addie down the hall. Looking down at himself, he immediately realized he needed to change his clothes before he went out into the hall. He rushed back into the bedroom and found another set of clothing that would fit him.

While he changed, he glanced at the clock and, with little surprise, he noted it was already six in the morning. Shoving the bloody clothes into a drawer, Alan rushed to the front door and opened it. The plush carpet in the hall didn't show his footsteps, so he couldn't easily figure out which way he had come.

"If you are in such a hurry to know, I'll just show you, slave."

The djinn had been silent for so long. When his words scratched across his brain, Alan froze. Throwing the door shut, he locked it and as the darkness came again, he sank to the ground. He felt frozen with fear, suspecting he was about to watch Addie's murder at his own hands.

Bound by Blood

HE FELT WEIGHTLESS, FLOATING, with no tether pulling him in. The feeling was freeing at first, but his mind felt muffled until he suddenly heard someone else's thoughts. He was standing in front of a mirror, but it wasn't him in the reflection. The shock was not as great this time, but it was still disorienting as the woman bent and splashed water on her face.

When she looked into the mirror again, Alan could tell she was in some sort of rest stop bathroom. His mind raced. There weren't any rest stops in Agra Heights. He couldn't be sure where she was. The bathroom was dim, and the woman looked tired, as if she were just getting off a late shift. Her name tag said "Tammie" and she wore a waitress uniform.

Alan took a moment to be thankful it wasn't Addie in the mirror, while also knowing something horrendous was about to happen to this hardworking woman, when she was just stopping to use the bathroom. Something in his mind tried to force Tammie to walk away, to get out of the bathroom. But she sighed and pushed her curly blonde hair from her face. She swiped at the smudged mascara under her eyes.

A clanking sound from behind her made her head come up quickly. She squinted into the mirror, looking over her shoulder. At first, she saw nothing, and Alan could feel Tammie's mind dismiss the noise.

But then a screeching sound seemed to slide along a stall wall. Goosebumps rose along the woman's skin, feeling like Alan's own skin.

"Who's there?" Tammie demanded.

Run! Just run! Alan tried to press into her mind. Even though he knew what he was experiencing was in the past, something he couldn't change, only be audience to, he couldn't stop trying. He couldn't stop himself from wanting to change the moment, to prevent what he was certain was coming.

Tammie didn't turn, but she looked in the mirror, studying the bathroom stalls behind her.

"Whoever you are, this isn't fucking funny. Just come out. I'm tired and not in the mood to be messed with," she called.

A dark shape took form as a person stepped forward. The movement caught Tammie's eye, and she spun to watch. Before she could make out the person in the stall, she turned and ran for the door. But she wasn't fast enough.

Alan felt the impact as Tammie's head was thrust against the bathroom sink. Stars exploded in his vision, Tammie's vision, as her body rebounded and tumbled backward. Alan steeled himself for what she would see next as her vision cleared and she could more clearly see the person in the bathroom with her. The orange glow of the djinn's eyes became more pronounced, and Alan could feel the confusion in Tammie's mind.

"What...are...you?" she tried to say, but her speech was confused and mumbled.

Alan's face, or the djinn's face, as he had thought of it, was barely visible. Just the glow of the inhuman eyes. Tammie was confused, from the blow to the head, and also by the supernatural look of what was attacking her. That confusion stopped her from fighting back right away. Alan tried to push her to do something, to strike out, to get away. But as before, he was only a bystander in the memory he was forced to live through.

"Always the boring questions. Who are you? What are you? As a species, you haven't evolved very far in five hundred years."

The voice sounded like Alan, but it was hollow, no inflection or emotion behind the words. They fell onto Tammie, like heavy stones being thrown into a pool. Her confusion deepened, but suddenly her fight-or-flight instincts could be heard above the thundering of her heart. Her scream was loud and high, the echo bouncing around the high ceiling of the bathroom building. She kicked, trying to push herself back, away from the djinn.

The djinn watched her, his face impassive, until she was close to the door again. Carefully, he stepped around her flailing body and reached the door before she could. As she rose onto her knees to grab the door handle, the djinn flipped the lock and moved to stand in front of her. In a lover's caress, the djinn's hand came up and his fingers ran down her cheek.

Crouching, the djinn grabbed Tammie by the upper arms and yanked her to her feet. Alan could feel through her mind and recognize the strength of the djinn. He knew his body, and it wasn't as strong as it seemed now.

As Tammie struggled, the djinn's grip tightened, sending a chilling shock through her body. Alan could tell his touch felt unnaturally cold, as if it had sapped the warmth from the very air around them. He felt confused, not understanding what was happening to his body. The bathroom lights flickered intermittently, casting erratic shadows that distorted across the walls.

The djinn's eyes glowed with a malevolent orange light, and he leaned closer, his breath icy and unsettling against her ear. "You don't understand, do you?" His voice was a hollow whisper, yet it resonated with a disturbing clarity. "This is more than fear. It's a lesson in anguish."

Alan knew the djinn was feeding on it all, every emotion that bled from Tammie's body.

Suddenly, the lights went out completely, plunging the room into a stifling darkness. Tammie's breath became visible in the cold air, fogging up in frantic puffs. The djinn moved silently, his form barely discernible in the pitch-black room. Her breaths quickened, heart pounding as she felt his presence closing in from every direction. Despite her desire to flee, she remained motionless in her current position.

Alan recognized that this attack differed from the previous. With the first victim, the djinn did nothing otherworldly. Now he controlled the power, and his presence was more intense. He was changing Alan's features instead of just talking through him.

Without warning, the djinn's hand gripped Tammie's chin, yanking her head back sharply. His breath was icy against her neck. "Your suffering is just beginning," he murmured, his voice a cold promise. His words were like a curse, wrapping around Alan's mind and tightening.

Tammie's eyes darted around in the darkness, catching flashes of the djinn's glowing eyes and the faint, eerie smirk on Alan's face as the djinn feasted on her fear. As during the first attack, Alan begged in Tammie's mind for her to close her eyes, to run, to fight. But the woman became lost in the fear and despair the djinn was creating.

The darkness further enveloped her, and the djinn's hand slid down her throat until he was squeezing, cutting off her oxygen. Tammie's hands flew up, and she scratched at the hand and arm, Alan's arm. Her nails dug in and tried to rip the flesh away, but nothing deterred the djinn from his plans.

Despite the darkness, Alan didn't miss the flash of the blade as the djinn sliced at Tammie's body. He felt the stinging pain that flew through her nerve-endings. She attempted to scream, but the djinn continued to hold her close by her throat. Her vision darkened, and Alan hated knowing what was coming at the same time as he begged for it to be over.

When he startled awake, he was in the same place, against his front door. Lying still, he waited through the nausea that swamped him. The woman, Tammie, was another innocent soul that the djinn took from the world while inhabiting Alan's body. He felt helpless. Sitting up, he could see the black bottle, still sitting on the kitchen counter where he had put it out of Addie's reach.

Cleaning the blood from the perfectly clean condo took the rest of his morning. Once he felt sure that there was nothing left for Addie or her father's men to find, he stepped into the hottest shower his skin could handle. Steam billowed around him, and he leaned against the tile wall as the water turned pink around his feet.

Tears pricked Alan's eyes, and he badly wanted to curl up into a ball and cry. However, he knew if stopping the djinn was a possibility, it would be up to him. The djinn had gone quiet, as if he became dormant after he tortured Alan, soaking up all the sorrow and devastation.

In the silence, Alan tried to think back on his research. Nothing he'd had the chance to read pointed toward the type of monster he was dealing with. He toweled himself off, feeling the fear from Tammie shake his body again. Gooseflesh broke out across his skin, and he quickly pulled on a set of clean clothes.

A soft knock at his front door made Alan freeze. He was on his knees next to the bed, making sure the trash bag was hidden. The knock came again. Taking a deep breath, Alan worked to steady his heartbeat, as if someone else would hear it if they were nearby. At the door, peering through the peephole, he pressed his forehead against the wood. When he swung open the door, Addie stood on the other side with a wide smile and two cups of coffee.

The Weight of Confession

"Morning!" Addie walked into the condo without being invited. "I know I said I'd stay in for the day, but I figured we could hang out here while you make yourself at home?"

Her look was hopeful, and Alan just nodded and tried to force a smile onto his face. While Addie went to the kitchen, talking about making breakfast for them, Alan scanned the room. It would be so easy for him to miss something that would incriminate him. Addie moved around, pulling food out and started prepping on the counter where the djinn's bottle was.

Alan casually grabbed the bottle and went to his room. Putting it on the top shelf in his closet, he felt a sense of relief to not see it. He knew hiding the bottle didn't change what was inside him, but he needed space from the physical reminder of his possession.

When he entered the main room again, he found Addie had turned on the flat screen TV that sat in the living room with the large couches. He was moving toward the kitchen when the words 'Breaking News' caught his attention. Spinning, he watched as the screen flashed to a news reporter standing in the early morning drizzle, holding a microphone, with police activity happening behind him.

The tendrils of recognition slipped through his mind. Alan wasn't sure if it was the djinn projecting into his memories again or if he himself really realized where the reporter was standing. Behind the man was a rest stop bathroom building. It looked as dingy outside as Alan remembered from the inside. The reporter was holding an umbrella to protect himself and his equipment from the downpour.

"A source who didn't wish to be identified tells us this seems to be the work of a serial killer. A serial killer that the police haven't come to the public about. Our source, who is close to the information, believes there is a composite sketch that the department is working off of to find the killer. Though there seems to be no motive and there have been multiple victims, there are no connections between them."

Alan couldn't move. Behind him, he could hear Addie humming to herself, and the sounds of a pan moving on the stove. He could smell the onion she had chopped. His senses seemed in order, but he couldn't move his feet. He couldn't find his way to the remote to stop hearing what the reporter was saying.

"It's just horrible, isn't it?" Addie's voice startled Alan, and he could finally turn away.

"What?" he asked.

"The women. Hadn't you heard? This has to be like the seventh victim in the last few months."

Seven? Alan had only had two memories from the djinn. He hadn't been possessed long enough to kill seven women, had he? He thought about his missed time. No, he was certain it couldn't be more than one woman a night.

"They don't know who's doing it?" he asked.

Addie shook her head and turned back to the stove. That gave Alan some relief, but he knew there was no way he wouldn't be found out eventually, knowing he came back to his condo covered in blood. And who was going to believe that he had a demon inside him, forcing him to kill helpless women?

"What's with this sketch they're talking about?" Alan asked.

"First I've heard of it. This guy...it's remarkable what he's been able to get away with."

She was mixing something in the pan, and it smelled better than any breakfast Alan could remember. His stomach growled loudly, and Addie flashed him a smile over her shoulder.

Motioning toward the breakfast bar, Addie set down plates. She sat next to him, but instead of eating, she turned toward him and touched his arm.

"Alan, I'm sorry. This all must be a lot for you. The condo. The job. If you feel overwhelmed, please just tell me, and I can sit in my condo while you adjust."

Alan turned and took a bite of the fluffy eggs, onions, red peppers and spinach. He closed his eyes and chewed quickly, before saying, "Nothing about this food is overwhelming. I haven't eaten this well in a really long time. I can't be upset about that."

They ate in companionable silence. Once finished, they washed the dishes together and Alan gave Addie the information she wanted about his past. Although it wasn't as interesting as she may have hoped, she was satisfied to understand who he was and why he was sleeping in the alley across from her condo building.

The news continued in the living room, covering the weather, traffic, and other top stories. It circled back to the murder in the rest stop bathroom, and Alan had to hold in his cringe.

"We now have the composite sketch the police have compiled from previous witnesses. If you see this man, do not approach him. He is considered armed and dangerous. Call 911."

Alan had to look. He had to know before Addie saw. Pretending he was picking up something from the coffee table, he focused on the screen. And he felt confused. It wasn't his face on the sketch. The man in the sketch didn't resemble him even slightly. The man had blond hair that flopped over his face. He had a large beaked nose.

Alan studied the screen, and slowly, the truth dawned on him. He had seen the man before. It was the man who had rushed away from him after apologizing and leaving him the bottle. Alan collapsed onto the couch, unable to stand any longer. The sketch disappeared from the screen, and he tried to take a deep breath. His body was trembling. He wasn't sure if the reaction was shock or relief.

He was also angry. Relived that no one seemed to have put him at the scene of the two murders his body was used for. But so angry to realize the man with the bottle knew *exactly* what he was doing when he left it in front of a homeless man. It was just one solution Alan had read about in the library. Something he didn't believe he was capable of doing to another human being.

The only way the man had found to get rid of the possession was to pass the bottle along to another human being. The understanding that the man didn't find another way hit Alan hard. He slouched on the couch, dirty dishes and Addie forgotten.

The news channel went to an infomercial that was loud and obnoxious. Alan barely noticed when Addie entered the room and turned down the volume before switching the channel. She sat across from Alan and studied him. When he finally looked over at her, her beauty struck him again. Her face was a mask of concern and at that moment, Alan knew she was the only friend he had in the entire world.

"What do you think makes a person do things like that?" Alan nodded toward the TV.

"Murder? I don't know. I don't believe people are just born bad. But something is broken in them."

"What breaks them?"

Addie tilted her head, her brow creasing as she thought about her answer. "I guess there are different variables in that. Abuse, childhood trauma, something wrong psychologically."

Alan held his breath for a moment, as his body trembled. He felt broken, but not because of the reasons Addie listed. The need to tell her, to confide in her, sat in his chest. He needed someone to know him, what he was facing, and believe him. "Do you believe outside powers could cause someone to do those kinds of horrendous things?"

"Outside powers? Like someone threatening him?"

He shook his head. "No. Something worse, something that can't be stopped."

Addie just stared at him, confusion clear on her face.

"Do you believe in the supernatural?" Alan asked, breaking the uncomfortable silence.

"Supernatural, as in witches, vampires—"

Alan cut her off. "Demons, possessions, forces beyond your control."

Addie laughed, but stopped when Alan just looked down at his feet. "Oh, you're serious. Well, to answer the question, no. I don't believe in those types of things. I believe if I can see it, touch it, it's real."

"And if I told you I know differently?" Alan's voice was just above a whisper.

There was a long stretch of silence before Addie responded. "I'd say I believe you."

On the Edge of Control

ALAN DIDN'T HAVE THE words to explain what he wanted Addie to know. He convinced her that an outing to the library would help, and she agreed. He wore dark sunglasses that he found in his condo and a baseball cap pulled low. Despite the sketch not showing his face, he still couldn't get past the feeling of being recognizable on the street.

The librarian's face expressed surprise when they walked into the library. The last time Alan had come into the building, he had been dirty from the street and slumping in a corner, trying to stay out of the way. Now, he walked in with his head held high, with Addie at his side.

Without asking, Alan remembered where the books were that he had looked at before. He went directly to the section and pulled a stack before guiding Addie to a table. Flipping through the first book, he laid it open, pointing to the most important passage. She leaned over, and he watched as emotions flitted across her face.

"A djinn? What are you trying to tell me?" she asked.

"Do you believe this could happen? That this could be real?"

Alan didn't know if she would believe him, but something deep inside told him he could trust her. And he wanted to trust this beautiful woman who had captured his attention. He also wanted to protect her from what he was becoming. If the djinn knew how he was feeling about Addie, he was sure she would become a target.

"These are superstitions, from ancient civilizations. They seemed to believe these things could or did happen. But I'm not sure I would believe that now without some sort of proof," she replied.

Alan stared down at the illustration in the book. It was a history book, and Addie was correct that it talked about the beliefs of ancient civilizations from around the world. Nothing had been recorded about the djinn in modern times. He had to wonder if that wasn't because the people he possessed died in the process.

A light touch on his arm brought his face up to meet Addie's gaze. Her eyes were warm, and she studied him closely. It was a look of someone who cared, and Alan wished it was as easy as taking her into his arms and letting her know what he was feeling. But the knowledge of the djinn inside his body stopped him from letting the emotions spill from him.

"Proof. Sometimes proof of something like this isn't something you really want to see," Alan said, snapping the book shut.

"Al, whatever you're trying to tell me or show me, just say it. I'll believe you. I trust you."

"You shouldn't."

With that, he turned and placed the book on a cart to be returned to the shelf. He walked toward the door, not looking back, but feeling Addie's presence close to him. They exited the library, and the sun was breaking through the storm clouds as it rose high into the sky.

"Badora Haddad?"

A small woman stood at the bottom of the steps that led to the library. Alan stopped and stepped in front of Addie. Looking up and down the street, he didn't immediately see a threat.

"Yes?" Addie asked, stepping around Alan.

"Addie." Alan's voice was quiet, trying to call her back to him.

As soon as the woman could clearly see Addie, she smiled and nodded her head, before turning and walking down the busy street. The pounding of feet from behind them was the only warning Alan had. He dropped low and pivoted just as a fist sailed through the air above him. Addie screamed when a second man appeared and grabbed her around the waist.

The djinn immediately rose, cackling inside his mind as he fed on the rage that was flowing through Alan's veins. With little thought, Alan threw a vicious fist toward the gut of the man that had tried to strike him. The air whooshed from the attacker's mouth, and he doubled over. Alan took a step up, bringing his knee with him, connecting it solidly with the man's face. When the man collapsed, he rolled down the last five or six steps to land on the sidewalk.

Alan spun and found Addie fighting with all her might against two men. One was holding her around the waist and the other was trying desperately to control her legs. Again, as if his body was operating without his express instruction, Alan sprinted up the steps, just as the men disappeared around the corner of the library with Addie.

When he rounded the corner, one man was waiting for him. Alan dodged, but not fast enough. The punch landed on his shoulder and spun him slightly. The pain barely registered through Alan's anger. He knew the emotion was being amplified by the djinn's presence, but at that moment he was okay with it.

The man pulled a knife from a pocket and as the blade was exposed, Alan stepped back to give himself room to fight. The man didn't wait, as he tried to stab him in the gut. Alan spun and caught the man's arm under his, using a move he had never practiced or been taught. With a brutal upward movement, a cracking sound could be heard, and the assailant cried out in pain.

The knife clattered to the concrete, and Alan shoved the man away and ran along the building. The walkway led to a back exit from the library and the lot where employees normally parked. When he got to the lot, he found the second man, dragging an unconscious Addie along the asphalt. A black sedan sat with the doors open and a fourth man sitting behind the wheel.

"He's coming!" the driver cried out.

Pouring on the speed, Alan reached them just as the man dropped Addie. He tried not to wince at how her head hit the ground. The man put his hand into his jacket, but before he could produce a weapon, Alan tackled him, taking him down to the asphalt. Quickly, he was able to straddle the man, pinning him to the ground as he rained punches down on his face.

The scene was too much for the driver, and the dark sedan screeched out of the lot, leaving the man to the barbaric beating from Alan. Blood coated the man's face and Alan's knuckles, but he didn't stop. The attacker didn't fight back. His eyes had rolled back into his head and his body had gone limp.

"Al..." The plaintive voice from behind him made Alan freeze.

His lungs burned, and he gulped in air. The red from his vision cleared, and he looked down at the man under him. His face resembled frozen hamburger meat that had been left out to thaw. Blood leaked from his nose, mouth and many wounds from Alan's beating.

"Al, please..." Addie's voice came again, and Alan scrambled off of the man.

Addie was still on the ground, but she had lifted part of her body up so she could see Alan. There wasn't fear on her face when she looked at him, only gratitude. He looked at his hands that were covered in red and down at Addie. She held a hand out to him, deciding for him.

Crouching, he slid one hand under her knees and the other around her back. As he lifted her into his arms, she let her head fall to his shoulder. Her arms came around his neck and she held on like he was her lifeline.

"That was succulent, slave."

The djinn's voice caused Alan's steps to falter, but he kept his hold on Addie.

"Watching over this woman brings me much joy. I think I shall allow you to continue this work," the djinn said.

The destruction left by Alan's fists sickened him. He didn't want to behave in ways that brought happiness to the djinn. That wasn't who he was. However, a small piece of him was thankful the djinn was giving him talents he didn't have on his own. He wanted to protect Addie, however possible.

In the condo building, Alan headed toward Addie's door.

"Please, I don't want to be alone. Will you stay?" she asked.

Alan just nodded, not really able to speak through the lump in his throat.

Her condo was almost exactly how he pictured it. The feminine decor made the space feel less cold and more like an apartment with a lived-in feeling. The layout was like his, and he easily found the primary bedroom.

Putting Addie on her feet, he kept his hands on her upper arms until she seemed steady. Her eyes were a little too wide, and she seemed to tremble.

"Are you okay?" he asked.

"I just can't believe this keeps happening. I probably need to let my father know. Whatever his response to the message was, it wasn't strong enough."

"Do you think he'll agree to the terms to make the partnership?"

Addie's eyes flashed with anger, and he felt her straighten her spine. Alan stepped back, knowing she didn't need to be held up any longer.

"I will not be a bargaining chip."

A Leap into Darkness

ADDIE CALLED HER FATHER, and Alan waited in the living room. He could hear her voice rising as they argued. Khalid wasn't someone that was used to being told no. However, Alan didn't think Addie was someone that just lay down.

When the yelling stopped, he heard water running and imagined Addie decided to take a shower. Wandering into her kitchen, he rummaged through her cabinets until he found a teapot, tea bags and sugar. He couldn't be sure, but he felt like something warm could be comforting after the day she'd had.

Some time later, Addie came down the hall. She was in a robe tightly wrapped around her body. Her hair was still damp, and her eyes were red-rimmed. He wanted to ask her about the tears she had shed, but didn't want to pry into a life he had no right to be in.

She came into the kitchen and slid into a chair at the breakfast bar. He placed a mug of steaming tea in front of her, and she gave him a small smile of gratitude. Leaning against the opposite counter, Alan sipped at his own tea, watching her as she stirred a small amount of sugar into her mug.

"I guess you heard that," she said.

Alan shrugged. "Not everything."

"Can you believe he actually suggested we attend a meeting to discuss the offer of this marriage?"

"You didn't expect him to think about it?" Alan imagined someone like Khalid worried little about crossing lines. He got to his position somehow.

"I thought…I'm not sure what I thought. He's my father. You'd think he wouldn't want me married off to a rival gang. He doesn't even know this son that the proposal is about. What about love? What about knowing someone? I don't want to spend the rest of my life as a pawn for his power trip!" Addie's voice rose higher and higher with each word. Alan imagined she would be screaming in her father's face if he were in the room.

"Is this not something he would typically do in business? Do anything to get to the top?" he asked.

"Yes. That's how he's become who he is. And this probably seems foolish, but he's always just been my father. His business never really touched me. Sure, there's been money. Yes, I live in this beautiful building that my father owns. But beyond that, what he had done to become this larger-than-life man never really hurt me." She put her face in her hands and shook her head. "Maybe this is my punishment. I turned a blind eye for too long. Now, I'm going to pay for it."

Alan moved to stand next to Addie. He squeezed her shoulder softly. "You've been through a lot today. How about we order dinner in, and you go to bed early?"

Addie didn't put up a fight, so he chose a dinner spot and ordered enough food for them to share. She ate little, and Alan prompted her to eat a bit more before he packed it all into her fridge to be reheated later.

She moved like a ghost down the hall toward her bedroom before turning to look at him. "Will you stay? You can lie on top of the covers. It'll be appropriate. I'm just afraid."

It took Alan a moment to ponder the situation, but the fear on Addie's face and the tremble in her hand as she extended it made the decision for him. He took her icy hand in his, rubbing it to help calm her shaking.

Her bedroom was more of what he expected. It was decorated in soft colors and neat as a pin. Except for her bedside table, which had a large stack of books, many with bookmarks in them at some interval. He wondered if she lost interest in things quickly, or if her tastes varied so widely that she had to read multiple things at once.

She crawled under her blanket, and Alan helped pull the covers over her body. When he reached for the light, she shook her head. "Can you wait until I fall asleep?"

Leaving the light, Alan sat on top of the comforter on the opposite side of the bed. Addie curled into herself, but turned onto her side to face him. Her brow was furrowed as she tried to force her eyes shut. After some time, her breathing evened out, and Alan watched as her face relaxed, the worries of the day bleeding away.

He lay his head back against the pile of decorative pillows behind him. His eyes closed on their own and he didn't fight the feeling of comfort and calm. Abruptly, he felt the djinn waking and moving through his body, crushing the serenity. Slowly, his head rolled back and forth as he tried to fight the djinn back into the dark corner of his mind.

"This is perfect, slave. You've brought her to me."

The words tore through Alan like electricity, and he shot off the bed in a panic. The djinn cackled, and he grabbed his head as the sound became louder and louder.

Addie, sensing Alan's shift from the bed, sat up. "Al? What is it? What's wrong?"

He didn't have the words to tell her, to explain what she didn't want to believe. He had shown her exactly what it was, but she dismissed it as a legend. However, that legend was screaming inside his skull, the sounds echoing throughout his thoughts. When he opened his eyes and looked at Addie, she cried out and scrambled back.

"Your eyes! What's wrong with you?" she cried out.

She had a dresser with a large mirror on top. Alan moved until he could see his reflection. And what he saw scared him more than the sounds in his mind. His eyes, normally a deep blue, were glowing orange. He had seen it before, in the memories from the djinn. But the monster had never shown himself in this way before.

"I...I can't do this anymore," Alan said to himself, though Addie was staring at him.

Running from the room, he absently heard Addie calling after him, asking him to come back. But Alan couldn't risk it. The djinn was trying to fight to the surface, trying harder to become one with his body. He ran through the condo, not pausing until he got to the front door.

Snapping open the locks, he ran into the hall and weighed his options. He could go back to his condo, lock himself in. But the djinn had already proved a locked door didn't stop him from getting what he wanted. And the deep feeling Alan was getting in his mind was that the djinn wanted Addie now.

He ran to the end of the hall and found the door for the stairs. On the first landing, he looked down and up. They were only a few floors from the roof, and Alan ran up, taking two stairs at a time. In the fog of his mind, he could hear a door open below him and Addie's voice ringing out. The djinn rose and tried to stop his upward progress, but Alan fought through.

The door to the roof burst open, and Alan felt grateful that it wasn't locked. Turning his face upward, toward the inky black sky, he released a bellow full of pain and fear. The djinn slid along his consciousness, continuing the loud laughing, keeping Alan from hearing much else. At the edge of the roof, he looked down the fifteen floors to the street below. Despite the evening hour, there were people walking along, minding their own lives.

With shaky hands, he climbed atop the ledge. Once he was on his feet, he held his arms out to keep his balance. The wind whistled, pushing him from side to side.

"Al...oh my god, what are you doing?" Addie's voice surprised him.

Carefully, he turned, so he could face the woman he cared for. "I have to protect you."

"From what? What's happening?"

"You can see it. My eyes. I tried to tell you."

Addie stared at him, her eyes searching his face. "The djinn."

Alan nodded, glancing over his shoulder, down at the ground.

"This won't work, slave," the djinn whispered in his mind.

"Shut up!" Alan screamed, causing Addie to startle and step back.

"You cannot be rid of me so easily." The djinn's strength flexed as he spoke, and Alan knew it was only a matter of time.

"I'm sorry, Addie. I can't control him much longer. He wants you. He knows you're important to me. He wants..." He grabbed his head as the djinn fought to come free. "He wants to make me suffer."

"And suffer you will, slave. I will have her blood on my hands," the djinn said.

"No! You won't touch her!" Alan screamed.

He turned on the ledge again, his decision made.

"Al, please...don't do this. We can figure this out!" Addie cried.

The sands of time that flowed through him were coming to an end. He knew what he needed to do. With one last look at Addie, taking in her beauty despite the tears staining her cheeks, Alan stepped off the ledge and sailed into nothingness.

Unbroken Bonds

Pain pulsed through his body. Each fiber of his being ached. His eyelids felt glued shut, though he could tell that there was a light on the other side. Alan imagined there wouldn't be pain in death. However, he wondered if the horrors caused by his body, while possessed by the djinn, meant he would spend eternity in hell, burning in pain.

"Al? Can you hear me?"

Addie's voice wouldn't be in hell. That he knew.

"Nurse, I think he's waking up." Addie spoke again, her voice close to his head.

Nurse? Alan thought to himself.

"The doctors have reduced the medications that were keeping him asleep. He should wake up slowly and will probably be disoriented. Don't be alarmed if he doesn't know what's going on or recognize you, okay, honey?"

The second voice was one Alan didn't recognize. All the words were English, but he was having a hard time understanding what was happening. The last thing he could remember was deciding to protect the beautiful woman at his side by any means necessary. And the last choice he felt he had was to jump to his death.

Nothing made sense about Addie speaking quietly with the other person in the room. Other sounds came to him. A steady mechanical beeping sound came from somewhere behind him. He knew it had to be his heartbeat, and that made the confusion feel even thicker.

Another feeling came to him. A dark, menacing growl vibrated through his mind. The beeping behind him quickened, and Alan's breathing became labored.

"Nurse?" Addie asked, her voice laced with worry.

"It's okay. He's probably just coming out of sedation and feeling a little scared."

Scared was one word to choose. Terrified was closer to accurate. He had thrown himself from the top of a fifteen-floor building. His body should have splatted on the asphalt, without question. Yet, he had general pain, but he didn't even think he had any broken bones. There was only one way that was possible.

"It was never going to be that easy, slave."

Alan's eyes flew open, and he started to hyperventilate. Addie was right next to him, and she jumped to her feet to move out of the way of the nurse that was trying to calm him. Eventually, another nurse ran into the room, and something was put into his IV. A warmth of calmness floated over him and his panic increased, though physically he wasn't able to continue to flail. The medication forced his breathing back to normal and his eyelids felt heavy.

When he woke again, the realization that his attempt on his life had failed was already a solid understanding in his brain. Addie was still next to him, curled up in the chair, asleep. The feelings he was developing for her seemed to swell further. As he felt the djinn slither around his mind, he wasn't sure those feelings were a good thing.

He shifted in the bed, testing his limbs, and he let out a low moan. Addie immediately woke and sat up straight in the chair. Her face brightened as soon as she saw him awake.

"Al, oh god. Do you need pain medication? Are you hurting? Can I get you anything?" She fired off the questions as she rushed to his side.

Carefully, she took his hand in hers and pushed his hair off his forehead with her other. He grabbed her hand and in a whispered voice, he started his story. Everything spilled from his mouth as he told her the truth about the djinn and what he had made his body do. Addie covered her mouth with a trembling hand, though she didn't pull her hand from his.

When he finished, there were tears on his cheeks and his despair was a thick fog in the room. Addie stood up suddenly and paced. She touched one wall and then turned and walked toward the other. Alan stayed silent while she moved. He wasn't sure what else he could say.

"Your eyes...before you ran out of the condo. They were glowing." She seemed to be talking to herself rather than asking him a question. Her pacing continued, her hands running through her hair.

She finally turned and stilled, facing him in the bed. "That's how you survived the fall. The...creature...didn't let you die?"

Alan nodded. "He won't allow it. He needs my body."

"How do we get him out?"

Alan didn't miss how she said the word we. He didn't want her in danger, but knowing he wasn't alone made him feel like he could actually survive.

"The same way he ended up with me."

"Because the man gave you the bottle, and you didn't know it was cursed," she repeated a piece of the story he told her.

He nodded again. "I don't think I can do that."

"Weak, slave..." the djinn whispered in his mind. His entire body tensed, and he squeezed his eyes shut.

"What is it, Al?" Addie rushed to his side, covering his hand with hers.

"He's awake, but he needs to gather strength, I think. Saving me took too much of his power."

"Do not doubt me, slave. I will have you spill the woman's blood before you know it," the djinn hissed.

"Go away. You can't control me." Alan pushed the thought back at the djinn, silently communicating with the demon. He could feel the monster flex in his mind, but even Alan could tell he wasn't full strength.

"So, the only way to get rid of him, to get him out of you, is for someone to receive the bottle from you," Addie repeated the process again, as if she was trying to absorb it herself.

Alan just watched her as she stared into space, her thoughts seeming to flash across her face.

She fiddled with her fingers restlessly until suddenly she focused on Alan and nodded her head. "I know what we need to do."

Escape from Agra Heights

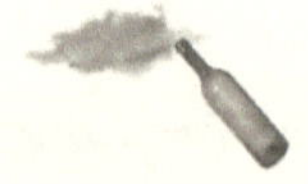

Two weeks later

Alan straightened his tie as he waited by the open car door. The suit was perfectly tailored for him, and it was made of nicer material than anything he had ever owned. The door of the condo building opened, and Addie swept out in a beautiful red velvet pants suit. She wore nothing under the jacket, with her smooth skin flashing in the deep V. Her heels clicked on the concrete as she made her way toward Alan.

"You look beautiful," Alan murmured.

"Thank you," she whispered back.

They kept their quiet conversation to themselves as her father and his men followed her. Alan and Addie's relationship had moved beyond professional, but until after the event they were attending, they weren't going public. It was all part of their plan. After the party Khalid required Addie to attend, Alan was going to take her away, and they were not planning on coming back to this city. Addie slid in through the open door, and Alan closed it.

Khalid approached him, as he was sliding his arms into his suit jacket. "Tonight is important, Alan. Badora needs to be there on time and on her best behavior. Can you do that?"

Alan nodded, but didn't trust himself to speak. The lie was on the tip of his tongue, but he worried Khalid would see right through him. The drug lord nodded his head and moved with his men to the waiting limo parked behind the sedan Alan would drive.

Alan waited until the limo pulled away before he slid behind the steering wheel of the sedan. Looking into the rearview mirror, he found Addie looking back at him.

An hour later, Alan pulled the car up a long circular drive, joining a long line of vehicles waiting outside a large mansion. People climbed from vehicles dripping in expensive jewels and clothing. Every window of the building was lit up and orchestra music floated across the wind.

It would be easy to forget what the family did to own such a home. What Alan couldn't forget was the reason he was bringing Addie to the party. Khalid had decided to discuss an engagement plan between Addie and the rival boss's son. Addie had raged and fought against the arrangement, but in the end, it made their decision even easier.

Once it was their turn near the front doors, Alan handed the keys to a valet and let Addie take his arm. Following Khalid's orders, Alan was required to stay by her side until the deal was struck. Even without the orders, Alan wouldn't have left Addie in this sea of sharks. Her hand squeezed his forearm while in her other hand she held a gift bag for their host, as her father had requested. Alan nodded, their plan set.

Alan could feel the djinn moving around his mind, and he only hoped he could hold the monster off a little while longer. Since Alan's attempt on his own life, the djinn had been weak, speaking his threats, but not attempting to take over his body. It had been easier for him to push the demon into a corner of his mind and live his life.

Now they would attempt to complete Addie's plan. She handed the bag over to Alan. Inside was the black bottle, the home of the djinn, decorated with a pretty bow Addie had created. It looked like a gift from a thankful guest to a wonderful host. But the only way for the plan to work was for Alan to be the one to hand the bottle to their chosen victim.

They walked together, Addie gripping his arm, through the throng of people that came to admire and worship at the feet of one of the most powerful men in the city. Khalid was striding through the room without a care in the world. He exuded power without saying one word. If they hadn't had a plan, Alan would have been tempted to curse him with the djinn.

"Badora, it's wonderful to see you," a man's smooth voice came out of the crowd as people parted and an older man stepped forward.

Addie squeezed Alan's arm tightly, the signal that this man was their host. "I'm only here at the request of my father. As I'm sure you're aware."

At Addie's nod, Alan held out the gift bag and waited for the man to take it with his own hands. He held his breath, unable to move from the spot until he was sure they had completed the process.

The man smiled brightly at Addie, as if she had given him a sentimental gift. His hand slid into the bag, pulling out the bottle. He handed the now empty gift bag to one man standing to his side. As Alan had done, the man wiped at the barely legible label. "I can't seem to make it out," he mumbled to himself.

Just then, the lights of the house went dark, all at once. Screams erupted from around them, and Alan knew it was time to go. Sliding Addie's hand from his arm, he twined their fingers together so he could pull her through the crowd. They hadn't gone far from the front door, and he could muscle their way through the confused crowd. Glassware crashed as people dropped what they were holding, or waiters panicked and dropped their trays.

A strangled cry rose from the middle of the room, and Alan felt a sudden release that caused him to pause and look around. Behind them, he could see the glowing orange eyes that had haunted him from the moment he received the bottle. For a moment, he was sure the djinn was focusing on him, but it turned away as the strangled cry turned into a prayer of some sort.

Alan didn't wait any longer. He pulled Addie from the house until they were running down the driveway. They had carefully planned their escape, parking a vehicle just a few blocks from the mansion. That car held their suitcases and all the documents they needed to start their new life, far away from Agra Heights, home of the djinn.

Epilogue: Echoes of the Djinn

THEIR LIFE TOGETHER HAD been perfect. With their new identities, they could stay off the radar until Khalid gave up the search for his missing daughter. Initially, the police suspected Alan, but once a letter from Addie surfaced, they could no longer argue she had been taken against her will. Some news reports called them a modern-day Romeo and Juliet, though Alan felt like that comparison would make no sense to anyone who had actually read the play.

At first, Alan obsessed over the news, as stories of the serial killer's rampage in the city continued. He didn't feel guilt over cursing the man with the djinn. The news about the party, stories of black fog and glowing eyes, confirmed that the man was possessed by the djinn. The man's soul had probably been black before the monster even infected him. What Alan couldn't get over were the innocent lives that were taken to feed the djinn's desires. Addie reassured him, but even her kindness didn't stop the nightmares.

They were married in secret and talked about having children. Addie became a teacher, working with at risk youth and guiding them onto better paths for their futures. Alan continued to work security, picking up private work on his own, until he found a steady position with a firm. It was honest work, and he felt pride in being able to provide Addie with everything she could possibly need.

Addie had helped Alan find a support group with other military members suffering from PTSD. Along with regular therapy, Alan was able to find peace in the life they were leading.

A few years had passed, and Alan's dreams had finally faded. He could never forget the women he had killed, even against his will. But he could push the memories back, so they didn't haunt him constantly.

One night, they cooked dinner together, laughing and dancing to music that played through a small speaker. Addie turned to have Alan try the sauce she was making, and he kissed her soundly when she got sauce on his upper lip. They were blissfully happy.

Addie turned and carried two plates into the dining room, so they could eat side by side at the table. Alan continued to stir the sauce when a plate crashing to the ground startled him and made him run into the dining room. He found Addie, frozen in place, staring at the table.

In the middle, a black wine bottle sat. As they watched, it fell to its side and rolled toward Alan, not breaking or slowing when it tumbled to the ground. He watched the black glass roll, and he could see an orange glow emanating from within. The last thing he heard before darkness swallowed him was Addie's scream mixed with the manic laugh of the djinn.

Twisted Tales of Familiar Faces

If you enjoyed this horror retelling of *Aladdin*, don't miss out on the rest of this horrifying collection!

Humbug (Scrooge) - Andre Gonzalez

Sweethaven (Popeye) - RJ Clark

Timber Beast (Paul Bunyan) - A.K. Hughey

Alice (Alice in Wonderland) - Audrey Brice

Wish (Aladdin) - Courtney Konstantin

Quixote (Don Quixote) - Stephen Wertzbaugher

Arturius (King Arthur) - A.K. Hughey

Steamboat (Steamboat Willie) - Courtney Konstantin

Strangled (Rapunzel) - Stephen Wertzbaugher

Dethroning Oz (Wizard of Oz) - Audrey Brice

Scorned (Hercules) - Z.S. Diamanti

Check out the entire collection at www.m4lpublishing.com

Join our newsletter to stay up to date with all upcoming releases at www.m4lpublishing.com

Author's Note

Thank you for reading Wish, a Twisted Tales of Familiar Faces novella.

Firstly, my appreciation goes to M4L Publishing, Andre and Natasha. Thank you for inviting me to be a part of the Twisted Tales Series. Your faith in my work has been an enormous encouragement.

To my fellow Twisted Tales authors, thank you for your camaraderie and collaboration. Staying connected about the series has been invaluable. Your creativity and enthusiasm have made this journey all the more enjoyable. (Except you Stephen...you know what you did. haha)

A special thanks to my TWS team for your unwavering support and dedication. Your encouragement and belief in my vision have been pillars of strength throughout this process.

To my family—my incredible husband and wonderful children: thank you for your love, support, and for the sacrifices you make that allow me the time and space to pursue my passion for storytelling. You are my inspiration and motivation, and without your support, this book would not have been possible.

Enjoy this book?

We hope you enjoyed this release from M4L Publishing.

Reviews are the most helpful tools in getting new readers for any books. We don't have the financial backing of a New York publishing house and can't afford to blast our books on billboards or bus stops.

(Not yet!)

That said, your honest review can go a long way in helping us reach new readers. If you've enjoyed this book, we'd be forever grateful if you could spend a couple minutes leaving it a review (it can be as short as you like) on the site you purchased this book from.

Thank you so much!

About the author

A Northern California native now settled in Oregon, Courtney is a writer fascinated by apocalyptic tales and the unraveling of societal norms. She finds joy in hiking, reading, exploring new destinations—especially cruises—and savoring time with family, all of which inspire her stories of resilience and survival.